THE
BODY
BOOK

The Lily Series

Non-fiction

Young Women of Faith

THE
BODY
BOOK

it's a God thing!

Written by Nancy Rue
Illustrated by Steven Mach

Zonder**kidz**

The Children's Group of ZondervanPublishingHouse

The Body Book
Copyright © 2000 by New Life Treatment Centers, Inc.
Illustrations copyright © 2000 by Steven Mach
Requests for information should be addressed to:

Zonder**kidz** ™

The Children's Group of ZondervanPublishingHouse
Grand Rapids, Michigan 49530
www.zonderkidz.com

ISBN: 0-310-70015-9

Published in association with the literary agency of Alive Communications, Inc., 7680 Goddard Street, Suite 200, Colorado Springs, CO 80920.

Art direction and interior design by Michelle Lenger

Printed in the United States of America

00 01 02 03 04 05 /❖ DC/ 10 9 8 7 6 5 4 3 2 1

Contents

What's Going On in There?

Sixty queens there may be,
and eighty concubines, and virgins beyond
number; but my dove, my perfect one, is unique.
(Song of Songs 6:8–9)

It's either happening already, or you've heard that it's going to:

- You're growing breasts.
- Hair is appearing in new places.
- You're sweating more.
- You've got the body odor thing going on.
- You're gaining weight or getting taller by the minute.
- Your friends are talking about starting their periods.
- You're giggling one minute and crying the next.

And in the middle of it all, you're looking in the mirror and saying, "Who are *you* and what have you done with *me?*"

This time in your life—between about eight and about thirteen years old—is when more changes are happening in your body than have ever happened since that first year (when you had to triple your weight, grow teeth, and figure out how to walk!). It can be a confusing time—a time when you want to shout to your body, "What's going *on* in there?"

Hopefully this will be a help to you: "What's going on in there" is normal. All these changes are because of something called *puberty*—and it happens to every girl and has since God first started making females. And probably every girl has had the same questions you might be having.

Girlz WANT TO KNOW

✿ *LILY: Everybody talks about "When you hit puberty . . ." What is puberty, anyway?*

Puberty is the time when your body starts producing two new hormones it hasn't produced before.

❀ *RENI: Swell. So what's a hormone?*

A hormone is a chemical that's produced in a certain organ or gland and is then sent to another part of your body to go to work. The two new hormones in puberty are *estrogen* and *progesterone.*

❀ *ZOOEY: I have chemicals in my body!? Why? What are they doing in there?*

They're slowly turning you into a woman.

Estrogen causes

- the development of your breasts (time for a bra?)
- the widening of your hips (think of it as curves . . .)
- the growth of all that extra hair in your arm pits and pubic area
- the production of more oil in your skin and hair (enter pimples and greasies!)
- the thickening of the hair on your legs (break out the razor!)
- your new interest in boys (They haven't gotten any less absurd—you just don't mind as much!)

Progesterone, along with estrogen, causes and controls

- your period

HOW IS THIS A God Thing?

You may find yourself wanting to ask God, "How come I have to go through all these pimples and all this embarrassing hair and all this crying that comes out of nowhere? Couldn't there have been a better way?"

In *our* minds, it might seem easier to wake up one day with a mature body, clear skin, and perfect coordination—but would that really be better?

People would also expect you to *act* like a full-grown woman—and where would *that* come from?

God made growth—all kinds of growth—a gradual process that takes time. The slow appearance of hair, the day-by-day way your breasts grow, the trial-and-error you have to go through with your emotions—that's all part of God's plan for you to have the time to get used to the idea of becoming a woman.

Hopefully, by the time you look in the mirror when you're eighteen or twenty, you're going to pretty much like what you see. The trick is to make it till then, right?

That's what this book is about: helping you to understand "what's going on in there" and giving you some hints on how to grow with it, physically and spiritually.

As always, there might be some obstacles, so let's try to get those out of the way right up front.

BODY BLOCKER #1:
I'm So Far Behind Everybody Else!

Maybe you're twelve and all your friends are getting their periods and wearing bras—and you still look, and feel, like a little girl.

If you have a brother who asks you, "Hey, Sis, when's the breast fairy gonna come?" or you just have the fear that you're never going to catch up, just remember these things:

- It isn't a contest! You'll get there at the right time for *you*.
- You are your own unique self. God has already planned how and when you're going to grow into that.

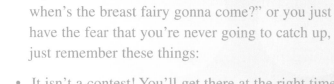

- Meanwhile, it's who you are inside that counts, anyway. If you have God-confidence, you're going to look, act, and feel just right. Concentrate on God and who he wants you to be.
- Enjoy being free of bras and maxi pads while you can!

BODY BLOCKER #2:
I'm So Far Ahead of Everybody Else!

Maybe you're twelve and are already in a C cup and have been having periods since you were ten. And maybe as a result, you feel like a freak.

If you're suffering from nicknames like "Betty Big Boobs," or other people are expecting you to act like you're sixteen because you look like you are, perhaps thinking about these things will help you:

- While you're wishing you didn't have such a well-developed chest, other girls are looking at their flat ones and wishing they could be so lucky! And yet, wishing won't make it so. You're going to develop on the schedule God has programmed in for your body.
- Remember that as your age group matures, you'll get less and less teasing because other girls will catch up, and boys won't think it's so funny to give you nicknames.
- Meanwhile, if it makes you feel more comfortable, wear clothes that play down your maturing breasts and curvy hips. It's not a matter of hiding who you are; it's a way to cut down on the teasing until everybody else grows up!
- Know that God loves you and has a plan for you, and that includes your womanly body. Let that give you the God-confidence to walk proud. Do not, under any circumstances, be ashamed of the way you're made. It's a God thing.

BODY BLOCKER #3: I Just Don't Want to Grow Up

Maybe the whole idea of wearing a bra, shaving your legs, remembering to put on deodorant, and—the worst!—getting your period seems really scary to you.

Don't feel alone. A lot of girls feel that way. Remembering these things might help you:

• Every girl goes through it, so you aren't alone. Share your fears with your friends. It'll bring you all closer together.

• God makes sure you have at least one adult in your life who is willing to help you figure this stuff out. Look around. Is it your mom? Older sister or other relative? A minister, counselor, nurse, or doctor? Knowing you have someone to go to who has been there (and done that!) will make you feel less afraid.

• It helps to think of puberty as sort of a path to better and better things.

• It's *fun* being a woman! We women get to have great relationships, experience incredible adventures, know never-ending love, and—someday—have babies. But to get there someday, you have to be *here* now.

• God's in it with you. He made the plan, and he doesn't expect you to follow it by yourself. Prayer helps—especially when nobody else seems to understand.

Your puberty years can be fun and even a little exciting if you start by really getting acquainted with where you are now.

✓ CHECK Yourself OUT

Under each question, circle the letter that best describes you.

1. **The hair under my arms and in my pubic area (that's between your legs)**

A. Hasn't shown up yet.

B. Is starting to sprout.

C. Has been there for at least a couple of months.

2. **My breasts**

    A. . . . what breasts?

    B. Are kind of a raised bump or sort of a pointy little mound.

    C. Have developed—the area around my nipples has gotten darker and/or I look pretty round and full.

3. **My waistline**

    A. Is the same as it always was.

    B. Feels kind of thick.

    C. Is a real waist now—actually smaller than my hips!

4. **My hips**

    A. Haven't changed.

    B. Have ballooned out! I feel fat!

    C. Are finally in proportion to the rest of my body.

5. **The hair on my legs**

    A. Isn't that noticeable.

    B. Has gotten thicker and coarser.

    C. Needs shaving now.

6. **When I take off my underwear**

    A. There's nothing on them ever.

    B. There's sometimes thick clear stuff on them or maybe something a little bit brown.

    C. I sometimes discover blood; yeah, I'm having periods.

Now let's see where you are.

If you have circled mostly A's, you haven't started puberty yet—and no matter how old you are, that's okay. It will happen! And when it does, by reading this book and asking questions and discussing your fears with an adult you trust, you'll be ready for it.

If most of your circled letters are B's, you're already *in* puberty. The hormones are working, preparing your body for womanhood. Even if you haven't started your periods, you're on your way. This can be the hardest time, but it doesn't have to be. Reading this book, asking questions, and discussing your problems with an adult you trust can make this part of your life a breeze—or at least a little less rocky.

If C was the letter you circled most, your hormones are fully operational! The worst is over—things are settling down. Before you know it, you're going to be very comfortable with your body, if you aren't already. For whatever you still may be questioning or struggling with, reading this book, asking questions, and discussing your problems with an adult you trust can help make the way smoother.

Talking to God About It

Let's start by praying. In the space below, write a letter to God, pouring out all the private, scary, embarrassing, I-don't-want-to stuff that you have inside. Just get it all out there—give it to God—and rest assured that he's listening. If that's hard for you, perhaps filling in the blanks in the open letter might help.

Dear _____ (insert your favorite name for God),

I know this whole puberty thing is your plan, but I have some problems with it.

For one thing, I'm embarrassed about_____.

Besides that, I'm kind of worried about _____.

And when you get right down to it, I'm just plain scared about

_____.

Will you please help me not to be too embarrassed or scared to ask _____ for help?

Will you please help me get answers to my question(s) about

_____?

And most of all, please help me to remember that I'm not alone—that you're there for me. I love you!

_____ (your name)

My most embarrassing moment in growing up so far has been when...

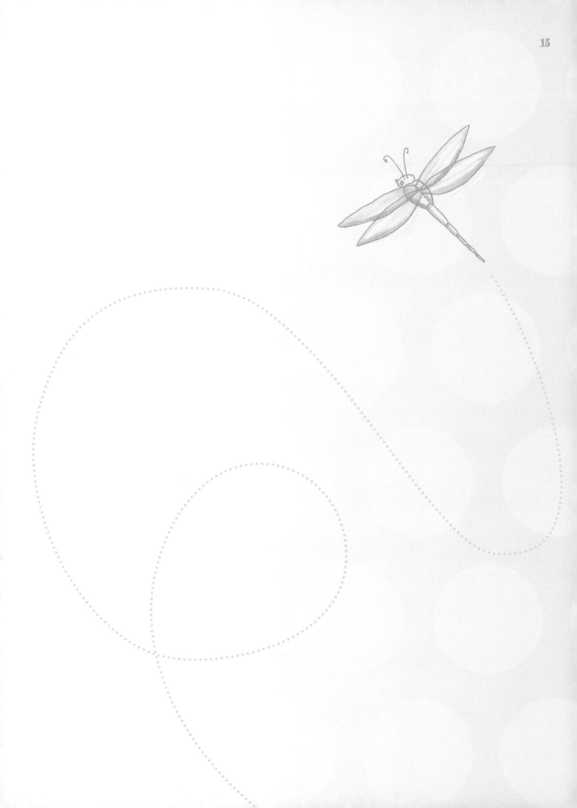

Attitude Check!

**Be happy while you are young, and let your
heart give you joy in the days of your youth.**
Ecclesiastes 12:1 (The Message)

It really doesn't matter whether you get through puberty with or without zits, with large breasts or a flat chest, with menstrual cramps or barely a trickle. No matter what, puberty's going to have its tough moments.

Maybe you'll get a pimple right on the end of your nose the night of the big dance recital.

Maybe you'll start your period in the middle of a soccer game—and the coach is a man.

Maybe some kid-with-no-tact will point out to you in front of your whole youth group that you ought to start shaving your legs.

The best tool you have for getting through it all will be your own *attitude*. Let's find out what that is right now.

✓ CHECK Yourself OUT

For each statement, circle the answer that's most true for you. Be honest!

A. My body tells me

　　3 When it's hungry, thirsty, tired, or sick—and I take care of it.

　　2 What it needs; but I don't listen to it.

　　1 My body tells me stuff? I never hear it!

B. When it comes to keeping clean

　　3 I'm there! I shower or bathe every day.

　　2 I do it, but it's a pain.

　　1 I wait until somebody makes me bathe.

C. Exercise is

　　3 Something I do a lot; it makes me feel great.

　　2 Something I do once in a while.

　　1 Something I hate! Just let me be a couch potato, okay?

D. Speaking of food

　　3 I eat a pretty healthy diet even when I'm not at home.

　　2 I eat healthy when somebody makes me, but I'd rather have junk food.

　　1 I don't eat healthy, either because I refuse to or because nobody insists on it.

E. When people talk about drugs, alcohol, and smoking being bad for your body

    3 I agree because I know that stuff'll hurt me.

    2 I just figure I don't need to worry about it until I'm grown.

    1 I think they're just trying to keep me from having a good time.

F. If somebody touched me in a way I didn't want to be touched

    3 I'd tell an adult I trust.

    2 I'd be too scared to tell anybody.

    1 I'd figure I must have done something to make that person think he could do that.

G. Next to the way other girls I know are developing

    3 I don't compare myself to them.

    2 I know right where I am.

    1 I think I'm a freak.

H. If I could change one thing about my body

    3 I wouldn't do it. I'm me.

    2 I could definitely think of one thing I'd like to change.

    1 I'd have a hard time picking out just one thing.

I. On the subject of periods

    3 I'm okay with it.

    2 I'd rather not think about it.

    1 Is there any way out?!

J. When it's time for bed

    3 I go because I like to get plenty of sleep.

    2 I stay up until somebody makes me turn out my light.

    1 I go to bed when I want—and I usually stay up late.

K. Emotionally speaking

    3 I have my moods, but they don't control me.

    2 I feel like my feelings are on a roller coaster a lot of the time.

    1 I'm in a bad mood a lot, and the people around me just have to deal with it.

L. I'm a girl and

    3 I love it!

    2 I mostly like it, but sometimes it's hard.

    1 I wish I were a boy sometimes!

Now add up all your points.

Before we talk about your score, please know this: your number of points does *not* determine whether you are good or bad, right or wrong, a sweetheart or a real terror! Your score will help you see where you are and why you're there. It will also help you find out what you might need to work on or get help with so your journey to womanhood will be smoother and happier. Everybody wants that, right?

If you have between 36 and 30 points, you feel pretty positive about your body. You respect it enough to take care of it, protect it, and like it for what it is. Keep it up! Look at those questions that you answered with a 1 or a 2 and pay careful attention when we talk about those subjects in the rest of this book. Don't let those areas pull your attitude down.

If you have between 29 and 20 points, you pretty much know what to do to stay healthy and to keep your body in top shape, but you aren't quite ready to do it all. Now would be a good time to look back at all the questions you answered with a 1 or a 2 and reconsider your attitude on those. Can you make it more positive on your own, or do you think you need to talk to someone about it? Read the sections in this book about those subjects extra carefully. Liking and respecting your body is going to make puberty—and the rest of your life—so much happier.

If you have between 19 and 12 points, you may really be feeling unhappy, maybe because you haven't made friends with your changing body yet. Now is a good time to start. Find an adult woman you really like and respect and see if you can spend some time with her. Try to find things about yourself that you like and focus on those things. Read this whole book very carefully. Pray, every day, as often as you can, that God will help you to love and respect the body he's given you to live in. It would be sad to grow up hurting, and you don't have to.

HOW IS THIS A God Thing?

Let's start with one of the great commandments Jesus gave us. He said, "Love your neighbor as yourself." Love other people the way you love yourself. If you don't love and respect who God made you to be, you don't know how to love and respect anybody else. Sounds empty, doesn't it? Jesus himself said to love and take care of that body. It's the only way you'll know how to care about anyone else's.

Are you going to argue with that? "But some bodies are easier to love than others!" you might say. Only society thinks that. God doesn't.

Pay Attention to Your Body

The second tool in making your attitude positive— next to believing God wants you to—is to pay attention to what your body is doing.

That doesn't mean getting so wrapped up in it that you don't think about anything else. So what *does* it mean?

Girlz WANT TO KNOW

✿ *LILY: My mother tells me to listen to my body. What am I supposed to be hearing?*

Your body gives you signals. If you're thirsty, your body is telling you it needs water. (Not a Coke or a chocolate shake—good old water.) If you're hungry, your body wants nourishment. (Not a candy bar or a bag of chips—nourishment—you know, something healthy.) If you're tired, your body wants rest. Are you going to bed early enough? Are you involved in too many activities? Do you get the idea? God made you with built-in warning signals that go off when your body needs something.

✿ *ZOOEY: If I ate every time I was hungry, I'd be the Goodyear blimp. I'm always hungry!*

Paying attention means learning when your body is telling you it's full, too. It also means making sure you're hungry and not just bored or stressed out. We'll talk about that more in chapter 6.

✿ *SUZIE: What if I can't give my body what it needs when it tells me? At school I get hungry way before lunchtime, and I always get sleepy before the last bell rings.*

Sometimes we need to adjust our bodies to the schedules we don't have any control over. Make sure you eat a good breakfast so you don't get as hungry before lunchtime. Try getting more sleep at night and more exercise during the day to keep yourself from wanting to doze off in class. If you work with your body, it will work with you.

✿ *RENI: I don't want to turn into some kinda hypo-whatever you call it, always listening for my body to make sure there's nothing wrong with it. That's weird!*

You're talking about a hypochondriac—a person who lives in fear of being ill and thinks every little ache or cough is a sign of big-time sickness. That isn't the same as paying attention to your body's true signals. If you do, you won't have to stress out over every little thing because there probably won't *be* little things. You'll be healthy and happy and able to concentrate on the fun stuff.

Just Do It

Here are three more tools for adjusting an attitude toward your body that isn't quite positive yet. Try doing each one, and see what works toward making you happier with the skin you're in.

Try this—Choose one of the areas you circled a 1 for on the quiz. If you had no 1's, choose a 2. Now, if you like to read, find a book in the library on that subject (exercise, diet, substance abuse, puberty, sleep, menstruation). If reading isn't your thing, find an "expert" on the subject—like a personal trainer, a nutritionist, a substance abuse counselor, a doctor, or a nurse—and interview that person. Learn all you can about the subject that is bringing your attitude down. Knowledge is great medicine for under-the-weather attitudes.

Try this—It's been suggested above, but now do it: find an adult woman you can really talk to. Your mom is probably your best choice, but if your mom isn't available, or for some reason things are too strained between you, use this checklist to help you think of just the right person. Your person-to-confide-in should be

_____ a grown-up, at least twenty-one years old

_____ a woman

_____ a Christian—not that women who aren't Christians don't know about growing-up-female, but since this is a God thing for you, you'll want someone who really understands that

_____ a person you feel comfortable with

_____ a person you respect—you would like to have some of the same inside-qualities she has

_____ a person who behaves as if she's very much at ease with herself— she isn't stressed-out and nervous or always complaining about her weight or her thighs or her gray hairs

_____ a person who is available to you

Have you thought of someone who meets all or most of those "require-ments"? Write her name here: _____. Give her a call. Tell her you'd like some help with some girl-issues and ask if you can get together. Using some of your allowance to buy her a soda when you meet would be a lovely touch. Oh, yeah, and always be sure to thank her for spending time with you—even in writing.

If you're still having trouble thinking of someone, consider these possibilities:

- someone at your church
- one of your teachers
- an aunt or other relative
- a counselor at school or the school nurse
- a neighbor
- a friend's mom

Try this—What's the most recent change you've noticed in your body? Are you suddenly developing "breast buds"? Has new hair appeared? Did you just get your period lately? Celebrate that change! Here are some ideas:

- Dip into your allowance, your birthday money, your piggy bank, and treat yourself to something fun.

- Invite a close friend over for popcorn and sodas to "toast" to your getting closer to womanhood—and celebrate her most recent development, too.
- Ask your mom if the two of you can do something a little bit special—go out and share an ice cream sundae or see a movie.
- Have your own private afternoon spa; take a bubble bath complete with a snack, some great music, and a scented candle (if that's okay with Mom or Dad). Luxuriate in the fact that you are female!

Of course the best way to make your attitude positive is to go to God with it. He's an expert at boosting your thoughts about yourself—the self he made for you.

Read Psalm 5 out loud for God. If it makes you think of a "psalm" of your own, write it in the space below. God loves hearing from you!

Lily Pad

The thing I like best about being female is...

Let's Get the Whole Period Thing Out of the Way

**Our sister, may you increase to
thousands upon thousands.**
Genesis 24:60

By far the biggest deal about puberty is menstruation—your periods—so let's go there first.

HOW IS THIS A God Thing?

When you have cramps or you've bled all over your favorite dry-clean-only dress or some boy teases you about the maxi pad he saw in your backpack, you may well ask, "How is this a God thing?"

I'm convinced God sympathizes with the discomfort and the inconvenience and the sometimes-embarrassment of having periods. But I also think he wants us to look at the good side of it—what having periods *does* for us. After all, if it weren't for menstruation, we couldn't have babies.

Let's look at how it works.

Menstruation (as the period-thing is called) is part of your reproductive system, your baby-making equipment. Inside your body there are several organs that make up this system. Check out the drawing, and then read about what each of these system parts does.

Ovaries are those almond-shaped organs that contain the eggs (or **ova**) you were born with. You started off with about 400,000 of them! Your ovaries make hormones—**estrogen** and **progesterone**—and once they kick in at puberty, they tell your ovaries—one on one month, the other the next—to let go of a ripened egg. That happens about two weeks before each period and is called **ovulation.** That **ovum** (singular for ova) will be caught up by the next part of your reproductive system, the **fallopian tubes.**

See the long "arm" that curves up to hold your ovary? That's a fallopian tube. It's about four inches long but only about as thick as a needle. On the outer end of each tube is a fringe called **fimbria.** The fimbria reaches out to move the egg toward the fallopian tube, and then tiny hairs inside push the egg along down into the uterus so it will be in place to meet a sperm.

If the egg became fertilized by a guy's sperm—meaning the sperm would meet the egg and break through the egg's outer shell—you'd be pregnant. If the egg isn't fertilized, it moves on down the fallopian tube to the **uterus.**

The uterus—also called the **womb**—is that upside-down-pear-shaped thing between the two fallopian tubes. It's about the size of your fist and its walls are made of strong, stretchy muscle. That's where a woman carries a baby before it's born; so right after the egg is released from your ovary, estrogen causes your uterus to build a lining of tissue and blood, just right for cradling an unborn baby. When you don't become pregnant, that lining has to be removed, so it's discharged through the **cervix**—a small opening about an inch wide in an adult woman—and out through the **vagina.**

Your vagina, of course, is the passageway leading to the inside of your body. It's four or five inches long, and it expands, since that's where a baby passes through as it's born.

As usual, God came up with the perfect plan for making sure unborn babies are taken care of in the womb (the uterus) and for getting rid of whatever isn't needed all those many months when a woman *isn't* pregnant. When you look at it that way—that we women get to have the babies—it just doesn't seem so bad. Besides, having as much information as you can get before your first period arrives will take away the rest of your fears. It's really pretty simple—girls have been doing it for thousands of years!

How Do I Know the First One's on the Way?

✓ CHECK Yourself OUT

See how many of these things are happening to you:

_____ You're between age nine and age eighteen.

_____ It's been about two years since your breasts started to develop and you started to get pubic hair.

_____ You've been noticing an occasional white discharge from your vagina. That will often happen for several months before your period actually starts and may even turn slightly brown.

_____ Your stomach is looking or feeling bloated.

_____ Your breasts feel tender and swollen.

_____ You have a sudden outbreak of pimples.

_____ You feel crankier or more easily moved to tears than usual.

_____ You're tired and don't feel like doing much.

_____ Your lower back aches.

_____ You feel like you've gained weight, but you still want to graze in the kitchen more than usual.

You don't have to have all of these symptoms before your period, and experiencing only one of them doesn't mean you should break out the maxi pads. But several of them together are a good sign that your first period could be on its way.

Girlz WANT TO KNOW

✿ *RENI: Okay, I gotta ask this: What is all that stuff that's going to come out of me when I get my period?*

Part of it's blood, but don't freak out. The rest is uterine lining and mucus from your cervix and vagina. It isn't "gross"—it'll probably be brownish-red at the start, go to dark red in the middle, and back to brownish-red at the end. You might pass some dark red clumps called **clots**, which are just parts of the uterine lining.

✿ *ZOOEY: Am I going to lose a lot of blood? Won't I get weak?*

Not to worry. You only lose between one and six tablespoons of blood during your period. Look at a measuring spoon and you'll realize it's just not that much. Besides, it doesn't come out all at once. It usually dribbles out slowly over three to five days, although some girls have their periods for up to eight, and others' only last two days. For most girls the flow is heaviest the first day or two and then it tapers off. It isn't enough to make you weak.

✿ *KRESHA: I heard you have to douche after your period because menstrual blood is poisonous.*

First off, menstrual blood isn't any more "poisonous" than the saliva in your mouth or the sweat in your armpits. It's a fluid that your own body makes, so it isn't poisonous to you. What a relief, huh?

Now, let's talk about douching. You've probably seen ads for vaginal douches. Douches are liquids designed to clean the vagina—except that the vagina is self-cleaning! It's like your eyes. Unless you have something stuck in your eye that needs to be flushed out, you don't wash out your eyes on a regular basis, right? You don't need to do that for your vagina either. The only time you should douche is if your doctor says you need to.

✿ *LILY: Is it all right to wash my hair during my period?*

Sure! There is no medical evidence that washing your hair during your period is harmful to you in any way. In fact, there is no *better* time to do it, because your body tends to produce more oil during your period. Go ahead and wash it. Look your best, because that will make you feel better, too.

✿ *SUZIE: A lot of girls tell me I won't be able to swim with the swim team when I'm on my period. What can I do? They're counting on me. Plus, it would be so embarrassing to tell my coach—he's a guy!*

Swimming doesn't do anything to hurt you when you're on your period. It's kind of hard to disguise if you aren't using a tampon; but with a tampon, no one will know you're having your period as long as you tuck the string into your suit. (More on tampons later.)

✿ *RENI: Okay—one more thing. What's with all the names for your period like "the curse" or "my friend." What am I supposed to call it?*

You left out "that time of the month" and "being on the rag" and "falling off the roof," not to mention "time to load up on Mickey Mouse mattresses."

The list goes on! Personally, I think it's the names we give to our menstrual period that make us dread it so much. Yikes, it's a natural part of what your body does. If you don't call it hate names, you probably won't hate it. Hey, tell it like it is—you're on your period. It's woman-time!

Get Ready!

One of the best ways to take the anxiety out of getting your first period is to be totally ready for it.

Just Do It

If you haven't already done this, why not ask your mom to help you pick out some supplies—preferably when your brothers aren't along on the shopping trip!—and tuck them away in a drawer next to your prettiest underwear. Add some great-smelling sachets and maybe even a feminine treat you get to have when the day arrives. Could be a tiny container of perfume, some amazing chocolate, a new pair of earrings, or a great pair of sweat socks! Make it something that will give *you* a lift.

Supplies

What kind of supplies do you get? The possibilities are almost endless. Maybe this list of "feminine hygiene products" (yeah, that's what they're called!) will keep it from being so overwhelming.

Pads

Most girls start with pads because they're easy to use, and they keep things pretty simple those first few months. A pad (we used to call them "sanitary napkins!") is just several layers of soft cotton made to absorb liquid. It has an adhesive strip on one side. You just peel the strip off and place that side against the crotch of your panties.

Pads come in more different shapes and sizes than most of us can keep track of. You might try a *thick* pad (like a maxi pad) the first few days, when the flow is heavier. Some girls like pads with *"wings"* that wrap around the edges of your panties for added coverage at the beginning. After your period slows down, you can always switch to *thinner* pads. Both thick and thin pads come with *straight* sides or with a *body-contoured* shape that some girls say are more comfortable. *Pantiliners* or *shields* are good for that last day or two when your period is no more than a drop here and there.

You'll also find pads that are *scented*. Menstrual blood does have a slight odor, and deodorized pads contain perfumes and

THICK

Wings

BODY~CONTOURED

Panti-liner

other chemicals to fight that. But scented pads do irritate some people's skin, so it's probably best to get the *unscented* pads and change them often to keep smells from being noticeable.

Tampons

A tampon is a narrow tube of absorbent cotton that's inserted into your vagina to collect the blood as it's leaving your body. Your vagina is flexible so it molds itself around the tampon, and then, because the tampon is like a sponge, it becomes larger as it takes in fluid.

Why use a tampon instead of a pad? It has its advantages:

- If you have it in right, you can't feel a thing.
- It's small enough to carry in your purse.
- There's less chance of odor than with a pad.
- You can't see it from the outside, even under a swimsuit.

If tampons are so great, why *not* use them? There are a couple of reasons:

- Your vaginal opening is narrow when you're young, so you may not be ready for a tampon right away.
- They can be tricky to get in. You might want to let yourself get used to the whole idea of even having periods before you try something *else* new.
- Some moms won't let their young daughters use them. If Mom says no, that's the end of it, of course; but it might help to remind her that using a tampon can't hurt you, it won't cause you to have cramps, and it won't make you sick. If you want to try tampons and your mother won't give her permission, go with pads for a while and bring it up again later. With a little time, she may change her mind. Meanwhile, respect her decision.

As you're gathering your supplies to put in your special drawer, you might ask some older girls what products they use. You could even get a few samples and wear them for a couple of hours (before your first period ever arrives), just to get a feel for what it's going to be like and what's comfortable for you.

Emergency Kit

While you're gathering supplies, put some, along with a pair of clean undies, in a small bag and tuck it into the bottom of your backpack or your school locker, if you have one. Why be caught off guard, right?

Dealing with It!

Now that you're prepared, you probably still have some questions. Even if you're already having periods, there might be things that continue to boggle your mind.

These issues, maybe?

Girlz WANT TO KNOW

❁ *LILY: What's it going to feel like? Am I going to feel like I've wet my pants all the time?*

Except for possible cramps, which we'll talk about later, you probably won't feel anything more than a faint trickle now and then. To prevent that "wet pants" feeling, change your pad every two to four hours. You don't have to get up in the middle of the night to change, of course. Just use a fresh one right before you go to bed and another one first thing in the morning.

❁ *ZOOEY: My mother is always telling my sister not to flush pads down the toilet. But how are you supposed to get rid of them?*

When you change your pad, roll it into a ball, wrap toilet or tissue paper around it, and pop it into the trash can. Public restrooms usually have a metal container in every stall just for used pads. Don't flush tampons or their applicators either, unless the box says they're flushable.

✿ *SUZIE: I'm a swimmer and I do gymnastics, so my mom said I may try tampons; but I'm kind of nervous. Aren't they hard to, you know, put in?*

Tampons aren't hard to use, but like anything else new, they take some practice. The first trick is to find the *type* of tampon that's right for you:

- *Cardboard applicator.* It has two tubes. One lets you insert the tampon smoothly; the other one pushes the tampon into place.

- *Plastic applicator.* It works almost the same way as the cardboard type. Some girls like it better because it's smoother.

- *No applicator.* This kind is very small and is just inserted with your finger. A lot of tampon beginners like these.

Then choose the right *absorbency* and *size.* Each type of tampon comes in junior, slender, regular, super, and extra-absorbent. Start small and work your way up. The best guideline is to use the tampon with the least absorbency possible without leaking accidents. If you're getting spots on your underwear after a half-hour, move up from slender to regular and see what happens. Some tampons come in boxes with assorted absorbencies for your whole period. Cool!

Once you've found the tampon you think might work for you, just follow the directions on the box, or talk to your mom or another adult you can trust.

That's it! Then be sure to change your tampon every few hours. If you run into problems getting the tampon in, check out this checklist:

- Are you aiming your tampon at a slant? Your vagina doesn't go straight up—it kind of angles toward the small of your back. Give it a slant and see what happens.
- Is your vagina too dry? Try some saliva or Vaseline on the tampon. Just don't use anything with perfume in it, which can irritate your vagina.
- Are you separating the folds of skin with your fingers? If not, you might just be pressing the tampon against the skin instead of into the opening.
- Does the tampon seem too big? Try a smaller size. If that doesn't work, maybe your body isn't ready yet. It may be a few more months, or even a year or two, before you can comfortably use them. In the meantime, find the most comfortable pad you can and relax. There's no rush!

❁ LILY: I tried a tampon, but it hurt!

That's probably because it wasn't pushed in far enough. Next time, just relax and push it in farther. If that doesn't work, pull it out and start over with a fresh one. You might also try using a tampon that expands out instead of up (there will be a diagram on the package). If you use one that gets longer as it fills up, it may have no place left to go!

❁ RENI: Can't a tampon get lost inside me, or—worse—fall out like in the middle of gym class?

A tampon can't get lost in there because the only opening from your vagina to the rest of your body is a tiny place in the center of your cervix. It's so small there's no way a tampon can get through it.

And there's not a chance of it falling out, either, if you have it in right. If you don't have it in right, you'll be able to feel it. If you do have it in there correctly, you won't even be able to tell it's there, and it won't come out until you pull the string. Your vagina is very flexible. It snuggles in around the tampon to hold it in place. There is also a ring-shaped muscle inside your vagina called the *sphincter*. Once the tampon is pushed past that, it also works to hold it in place. That's why it's important to push the tampon in far enough.

✿ ZOOEY: *Somebody told me a dentist can tell when you're having your period. How embarrassing!*

"Somebody" was pulling your leg. There will be nothing in your breath or your gums or your teeth that will give you away. Besides, would it really matter if a healthcare professional knew what was going on with your body? After all, it's natural, even for the most private person.

✿ KRESHA: *How will I know when my period is over?*

Good question! When you haven't seen any blood on your pad or tampon for several hours or maybe an entire day, you can be pretty sure it's coming to an end. Also, the color will probably change, too, from bright red to rusty brown. You might want to wear a pantiliner for a day or two after that, just to be on the safe side. Once you've had your periods for a year or two, they'll become regular and will last for about the same number of days each time. That'll make it easier to tell when you can shed the pads for another month.

✿ RENI: *So this is going to happen every month, right?*

That's right, until you're about fifty years old (except during the months you are pregnant, if that happens in your life). At first your periods might not be regular, but after a year or two they'll settle into a cycle of about twenty-eight days. That means that the time between the start of your period until the start of your next one is twenty-eight days—although for some girls it's as short as twenty-one or as long as thirty-five days. Get yourself a calendar and circle the day you start your period and the day you stop. Do that for several months and see if a pattern doesn't form. It's also a good way to be ready with supplies for the next one and maybe even wear a pantiliner for a day or two before you expect to start.

Talking to God About It

Make no mistake about it, getting your period is big stuff at first. Although you might have an understanding mom or big sister or other female friend older than you, it's good to take your fears, big or little, to the One who cares the *most* about you and understands every little anxiety that you think is lame but which is driving you nuts! Go to God with it. Want some help?

Dear God,
Someday, since I'm a girl, I'm going to get my period. Here's how
I feel about that, God, honestly and no-kidding:

_____

_____.

Will you help me with that? Will you (circle all the ones you need):

- soothe my fears?
- help me stop worrying?
- help me get prepared?
- help me find somebody I can talk to about it?
- help me see it as something exciting that's about to happen to me?
- make me a little more glad to be a girl?

_____

(add your own if you want to)
Thanks for loving me, God. Amen.

Lily Pad

If I could talk to my "baby-making equipment" in there, here's what I'd say to it...

When Your
Period's a Pain

Hear my prayer, O LORD; let my cry for help
come to you. Do not hide your face from me
when I am in distress. Turn your ear to me;
when I call, answer me quickly.

Psalm 102:1–2

Even if you haven't already started your period, you've probably heard the horror stories.

"I get killer cramps!"

"I get PMS so bad my whole family hates me!"

"I started my period in science class, sitting right next to Shad Shifferdecker. It was all over the seat—I wanted to die right there!"

They might be a little exaggerated to make better stories, but there's a lot of truth to these tales. You *can* hurt and get cranky and bleed at the worst possible times. It kind of makes you ask, how *is* this a God thing?

HOW IS THIS A a God Thing?

Not everything the Bible says about menstruation is all that helpful:

Leviticus 15:19 tells us, "When a woman has her regular flow of blood, the impurity of her monthly period will last seven days, and anyone who touches her will be unclean till evening." It goes on to say anything she lies on or sits on is unclean, too, and that whoever touches what she touched practically has to bathe in turpentine.

In Genesis 31:35, Rachel tells her father, "Don't be angry, my lord, that I cannot stand up in your presence; I'm having my period." And he accepts that as being perfectly logical. Yikes!

Isaiah (30:22) even compares destroying idols with throwing out a used "menstrual cloth."

Those Old Testament folks had a totally different view of menstruation than we do today. No wonder we sometimes still think of it as a "curse"!

But when it comes to pain and discomfort and embarrassment, no matter what the cause, God has comfort for us in his Word. Try these on for size:

Praise be to the God and ... the Father of compassion and the God of all comfort, who comforts us in *all* our troubles.

(2 Corinthians 1:3–4, emphasis mine)

Come to me, all you who are weary and burdened,
and I will give you rest.
(Matthew 11:28)

He tends his flock like a shepherd: He gathers the lambs in
his arms and carries them close to his heart.
(Isaiah 40:11)

For I am the LORD, your God, who takes hold of your right
hand and says to you, Do not fear; I will help you.
(Isaiah 41:13)

These verses weren't just written for people with fatal illnesses—they're meant for all of us, no matter what kind of discomfort we might be feeling. God understands all the growing-up stuff. It helps to know that.

PMS, Cramps, and Other Icky Stuff!
Girlz WANT TO KNOW

✿ *LILY: The other day my brother accused me of having PMS and said that was why I was so grouchy. What is PMS, anyway? Do I have it?*

PMS stands for premenstrual syndrome and it refers to the pattern of symptoms you get just before you start your period. PMS is a very real thing, caused by those hormones we've been talking about. Estrogen is a "feel good" hormone, and its level drops before your period. When it drops, so does your good mood! On one hand, PMS is helpful because it can alert you to the fact that your period will start in about seven to ten days. But on the other hand, PMS can be kind of a pain because it may involve any or all of these wonderful things:

- big-time hunger and thirst
- major fatigue
- feeling blue
- feeling blue one minute and *great* the next!

✿ *ZOOEY: My mother tells me all that bleeding won't hurt, but then I hear girls talking about cramps and I get scared!*

Some girls do get mild tummy aches right before and on the first day or two of their periods. Other girls—a very few—have pain they really have to pay attention to. Nobody knows exactly why cramps happen with menstruation, but they *are* usually normal and are nothing to worry about. We'll talk about some good ways to get relief in the next section. For now, relax. Cramps very seldom keep a girl from doing the things she likes to do.

✿ *RENI: I hear girls saying, "I must be about to start my period. I'm bloated." What does that mean?*

Bloating is a kind of swelling that happens when your body holds onto (retains) water. Usually it's in your lower abdomen, but you can also "bloat" in your breasts, hands, thighs, even your face. No need to stress about it, though. It goes away once your period gets under way. (More on bloat-relief in the next section.)

✿ *KRESHA: I started my period and had it for two months, and I haven't seen it since. Do I have to go to the doctor for that?*

You're experiencing irregular periods, as a lot of girls do their first year or two of menstruating. It's a new process for your body and it could take that long just to get into a pattern. Sometimes irregular periods are caused by other things, too, especially if you've been having regular periods for a while and then they get out of whack. Some of these causes might be

- Not-so-good eating habits—you know, like fad dieting, too much junk food, and not eating enough and then stuffing yourself
- Changing your location—maybe moving to a new town or visiting a place with a different altitude than you're used to
- Big, sudden weight gain or loss
- Big-time emotional upset or excitement
- An illness or injury
- Exercise overload—a lot of female marathon runners, for example, stop having periods all together!

How to Feel Better

But don't despair. All of the bummer things that go along with having your period can be relieved. Here's how:

Just Do It

If you've already started having periods or you're having the symptoms that show you will soon, check off the ones below that apply to you. Read about what to do to get some comfort, and then *do* those little things! There's no need to suffer. Life is not an endurance test!

Cramps

- Exercise at least three times a week, even when you're not having your period. That will build up your back and tummy muscles (more on that in chapter 7).
- Stay on a good, nutritious diet—all the time (more on exactly what that is in chapter 6).
- Once cramps hit, soothe them with heat—a heating pad, hot water bottle, hot bath, or one of those neat cloth bags filled with cherry pits that you put in the microwave.
- If all of that doesn't help, try one of the over-the-counter medications. The pharmacist can help you pick one out.
- If your cramps are so severe they keep you in bed or totally out of things, call your doctor. He or she may prescribe a medication for you.

PMS

- Again, exercise—walk, ride a bike, swim, play a game of tennis. Anything fun and active will lift your spirits, even if you aren't usually active.
- In addition to eating a healthy diet all the time (see chapter 6), snack on carbohydrates just before your period and for the first few days. Oatmeal cookies, pretzels, and popcorn work really well.
- In your regular meals, avoid too much sugar and caffeine. Go big on foods that are high in vitamin B—green veggies, whole grains, and nuts.
- Get at least eight hours of sleep a night.
- Know that the grumpiness and blues you're feeling are perfectly normal, but do try not to take them out on everybody around you. To say, "I can't help it! I have PMS!" doesn't quite make it okay! Instead, find somebody you can talk to about it. These feelings are real and they need to be expressed, but to someone who will understand.
- Pamper yourself in your free time when you're "PMSing." Listen to your favorite music. Soak in a bubble bath. Take a walk with your dog. Browse through old photo albums. Reread that favorite book you've read a thousand times. Be nice to *you*.

Bloating

- Get plenty of vitamin B all the time—meat, fish, poultry, whole wheat products, leafy green veggies, dried beans.
- Exercise regularly—even when you're not on your period (see chapter 7).
- Cut down on your salt, especially from two weeks before your period until it actually starts.
- It sounds strange, but drink a lot of water. Water helps flush out the stuff your body is holding onto.
- If bloating makes your breasts tender, try wearing a bra that holds them firmly—like a sports bra.

Irregular Periods

- Keep supplies in your purse, backpack, locker, or wherever you spend time. You'll want to be prepared since your period could sneak up on you!

- Eat right! (Are you seeing a pattern here?)
- Exercise regularly (another pattern!) but don't overdo it (we'll talk more about that in chapter 7).
- Give your body a chance to adjust to the big changes in your life. Most likely things will settle down in a month or two—within as well as without!
- Try not to let your weight change radically in short periods of time if you can help it. Yo-yo dieting, where you lose a lot of weight and then gain it all back and lose a bunch more and then put it back on—is really murder on your menstrual cycle, and a lot of other things as well.
- Of course, no alcohol or illegal drug use.

If you feel stressed out a lot—you know, anxious tummy, can't sit still, constantly worrying, maybe having trouble sleeping or concentrating—that can lead to funky cycles, too. Try these remedies:

- Find an adult woman to talk to about any- and every-thing. Start with your mom.
- Keep a journal to write in when things get to you. A fun one with a cool cover and some pens in your favorite colors will make this more enjoyable. Don't worry about spelling and punctuation and all that stuff—just "spill your guts!"
- Have at least thirty minutes of alone time every day to do something for you.
- Look at your schedule and see if you are doing too much. Do you really *have* to take gymnastics, ballet, *and* tap? Do they need you on the volleyball, track, *and* soccer teams all at the same time?

- Be honest with the people in your life. Don't let disagreements go unsolved or resentments build up.
- Go to God with everything. He wants to hear it all!

When Your Period Surprises You

Ask any woman if she's ever had her period sneak up on her when she had no pads or tampons within five miles and she'll say, "Yes! Oh, my gosh—let me tell you!"

It happens to everyone sooner or later; and contrary to how panicked you might feel, there's always a solution. Here are some tricks for avoiding embarrassment, collected from girls who've been there!

Tricks of the Trade

Make a temporary pad out of folded toilet paper, Kleenex, or paper towel to tuck into your undies.

If you're at school, ask the school nurse, a teacher, or a friend if she has a tampon or pad you can use. Don't be embarrassed. Your fellow women have been there, and they'll want to help.

If you're in a public rest room, there will probably be a coin-operated machine where you can buy tampons or pads. If you're penniless, don't be afraid to ask that nice lady who's combing her hair. Periods bond all women everywhere, and you are one of them.

If blood has leaked out onto your clothes, try the old sweater-around-the-waist trick. You can tie a sweater, shirt, jacket—whatever—around your waist until you can get to clean clothes and supplies. Some girls even suggest tying a sweater around your waist and then slipping out of your bottom part, rinsing it in *cold* water in the sink, and drying it with one of those hand blow-dryers you find in rest rooms!

If it's convenient, keep an extra pair of jeans in your locker at school or in your backpack. Then you're always ready.

A stain on your clothes will be a much bigger deal to you than to anyone else. Most people won't even notice it if you don't call their attention to it.

Think about it: how much time do *you* spend looking at other people's rear ends? If they do notice, most people aren't cruel enough to say, "Hey, Lily, you've got blood all over the back of your shorts!" Anyone who does is going to make a fool of *him*self, not you!

Just Do It

Hopefully, this is all starting to sound easier to you by the minute. Let's put the final comforting touch on it. Go through this reminder checklist and mark off the things you've done to prepare yourself for the whole period thing. Then go on with the other—more fun— parts of becoming a young woman.

_____ I have supplies at home, along with treats, for the big day.

_____ I have supplies at school, just in case.

_____ I'm eating right, exercising regularly, and getting plenty of sleep.

_____ I'm drinking at least six 8-oz. glasses of water a day.

_____ I'm making sure I'm not doing so many things that there isn't time for me, for alone time, for the small things I enjoy.

_____ I have an adult female I can talk to about anything.

_____ I'm keeping a journal.

_____ I go to God with everything, everyday.

You're set, girl. Now get ready to enjoy. Emerging into womanhood really can be exciting!

Lily Pad

Ask three different females for their most memorable menstruation moment!

Choose one memorable menstruation moment (it could be your own, of course) and tell about it...

Keeping Abreast

**We have a young sister, and her breasts are not
yet grown. What shall we do for our sister?**
Song of Songs 8:8

The thing people notice first when they realize you aren't a little girl anymore is your breasts. They're the first sign that you're changing—for the better!

All Shapes and Sizes

Breasts start to bud usually between nine and twelve years old. If yours are earlier or later, not to worry. Remember that God has each girl on her own growth schedule. In fact, nobody even knows how big your breasts will get or even how long it will take them to develop completely. We do know that they usually reach maturity around four to five years after they first begin to bud.

At first one breast might sprout more quickly than the other, but don't worry about turning out lopsided. They'll pretty much even out sooner or later, and you won't even notice that they're not exactly alike. (They never are!)

Don't bother comparing your breasts to other girls', because there are almost as many shapes, sizes, and even colors as there are women! Know your own breasts and learn to like them. They're you!

✓ CHECK Yourself OUT

Take a good look at your own breasts and then find out some fun things about them.

1. **My breasts**

STAGE ONE: _____ are not there yet!

STAGE TWO: _____ are just little raised bumps (called breast buds); the nipples and that circle of color around them (called the *areola*) are larger and darker than they used to be.

STAGE THREE: _____ are bigger than buds—in fact, they're sort of pointy and the areola and nipple are getting larger and darker all the time.

STAGE FOUR: _____ have the areola and the nipple in one mound that sticks out from my breasts.

STAGE FIVE: _____ have a full, round shape and the nipple is kind of raised; it's been about four years since I just had little buds.

Remember that each stage is a normal step in the development of your breasts. It's kind of fun to notice them growing and changing. If you have a little tenderness with each stage, don't worry. These are just "growing pains."

2.   **My breasts are** (circle the one closest to you in each pair)

round	pointy
high on my chest	low on my chest
pointed up	pointed down
pink in the areola	brown in the areola
blessed with nipples that go outward	graced with nipples that go inward
circled with little hairs around the areola	hairless

Looking at your own combination, think how many different combos are possible. God planned them all. Every breast is a beautiful thing that may someday be used to nurse a precious baby. Your breasts are a lovely part of your womanhood. Enjoy!

Bras

Once your breast buds start to appear you'll probably think about the bra issue. How do you know when, what kind, and what size?

Girlz WANT TO KNOW

❁ *SUZIE: I think I need a bra, but I'm not sure. How do I know?*

The best rule of thumb is—are you more comfortable with a bra than without one? You also might ask yourself these questions:

- Do you feel funky because your new breasts show through your clothes?
- Do you get self-conscious because you notice your breasts jiggling when you're active?
- Do your breasts hurt when you play sports?

If you answered yes to at least one of these questions, you're probably ready for a bra.

❀ *RENI: I answered no to all those questions, but all my friends have bras, and I feel like a geek—a baby geek.*

There's nothing wrong with wearing an A, AA, or AAA cup bra (more on that later) even if you don't "need" one. Or you can wear a pretty camisole to make you feel feminine and grown up. Tank tops and sports bras are great for that, too. It's no fun feeling left out, and in this case it's so easy to fix.

❀ *ZOOEY: I know I need a bra, but my mom doesn't really want me to grow up. How do I ask her without her getting all freaked out?*

Most moms are pretty impressed when their daughters surprise them with their maturity. Think about why you want a bra. Then go to your mom at a time when she isn't distracted and you two are alone, and state your case calmly and politely. (I'd suggest leaving out, "Everybody else has one!") Ask her if she'll go shopping with you and help you pick one out. I would really advise against going shopping with your friends and buying your first one on your own. Moms really like to be included in those important events—and it's never okay to go behind a parent's back.

If your mom says no, try putting a snug tank top under your shirt to help keep your breasts in place and keep you from feeling self-conscious until she changes her mind. She will—especially when she sees how mature you're being.

LILY: I wear a bra already, and my brothers tease me about it constantly. I know the boys at school are making comments behind my back, mostly because I'm about the first girl in our class to get one. I really hate feeling like they're all talking about my bra. They need to get a life!

Yes, they do, but there's not much you can do about that part. Some people just mature faster socially than others. Until they do grow up and "get a life," you might want to get your mom to buy you some bras in neutral colors to blend in with your skin. You might get them in a plain, smooth style without lace and bows. It isn't that you're trying to hide something—you're just avoiding being given a hard time. Sometimes, you just have to make it easy on yourself.

KRESHA: How do I know what size to get? I just don't understand all those letters and numbers!

Bra sizes have two parts: a number for the size of your rib cage and a letter for the size of your breast, called a cup size. You'll see combinations like 32A, 34B, 36A, and so on.

Here's how you figure out your size:

1. Measure around your ribs just below your breasts.

2. Find your rib number on the right.

22–23 inches	28
24–25 inches	30
26–27 inches	32
28–29 inches	34
30–31 inches	36

3. Now measure around your chest, right over your nipples.

4. Subtract your rib number (step 2) from your chest number (step 3).

5. Look for the number you get on the left below and you will find your cup size on the right.

−1	AAA
0	AA
1	A
2	B
3	C
4	D

6. Your bra size is your rib number and your cup size together. Write it here: _____. But don't expect every bra in your size to fit perfectly. Different styles will fit differently, so just use your bra size as a place to start looking.

You'll know a bra fits when it

- looks smooth under your shirt
- doesn't pinch you anywhere
- doesn't ride up in the back
- doesn't slide off your shoulders

Don't forget that you can adjust the size of a bra a little bit by moving the hook over one or two notches. Most bras also have an adjustment in the straps so you can make them snug but comfortable.

❀ *LILY: There are so many different styles I get totally confused. How do I know where to start?*

Just like everything else you can buy, bras come in so many styles, fabrics, and colors it boggles the mind! Colors and fabrics are just a matter of taste. Styles come in about four different types:

- "Training" bra—it doesn't actually "train" your breasts! It just helps you get comfortable with wearing a bra. Trainers come in A, AA, and AAA.

- Soft cup bra—it's soft and flexible and has an elastic band just under your breasts. This provides enough support for most girls in B cup or smaller. It's definitely comfortable when it fits right.

- Underwire bra—it has a curved wire sewn in under each cup to give girls in C cup or higher the support they need to cut down on jiggling. It's a little bit stiff, but it can still be comfy.

- Sports bra—just as it sounds, it's made for wearing while you're playing sports, running, and generally being active. It's basically a tank top that comes just below your breasts and is snug so they'll stay in place and be pain-free when you're on the go. Some girls feel so comfortable in sports bras they wear them all the time.

training

Soft Cup

UNDERWIRE

✿ *ZOOEY: When I do finally get a bra, I'm going to want to wear it day and night! Is that okay?*

Actually, there's really no reason to wear a bra to bed. It's nice to get a rest and kind of "hang loose" while you sleep.

Too Big! Too Small!

For some reason, a lot of American girls think they have to have the "perfect" breasts—round and

SPORT

full and spilling out of their blouses or small and perky and hiding daintily under their tank tops. Hopefully, you've figured out by now that the perfect breasts for you are the ones you have.

The tough part comes in when other people aren't content to leave your breast size alone! Have you heard these complaints or had them yourself?

"I'm so flat-chested, everybody teases me about it. I feel like a boy!"

"If the breast fairy doesn't come soon, I'm going to save up and buy one of those increase-your-bust things I see in the back of magazines."

"I get so sick of having nothing up top, I stuff Kleenex, washcloths, anything I can find in my training bra so at least I'll look normal!"

"I have the biggest breasts on the planet for a girl my age. Nobody in my class wears a C cup. The boys call me Dolly Parton, and I hate that!"

"I'm embarrassed to take my bra off in front of my friends in P.E. or at sleep-overs because I have these weird hairs around my nipples. It makes me feel like I'm part male."

Even if adults or your girlfriends don't think your problem is such a big deal, it can be painful for you. That's when the best One to go to is God.

Talking to God About It

As always, it's good to just go to your quiet place and pour it all out to God—out loud, in your journal, or in your head. If you need some help to get you started, here's a God-conversation starter.

> *Dear _____ (your favorite way of addressing God),*
> *I'm having some problems with this breast thing. I know I'm supposed to like my body just the way you made it, but I need you to guide me on that. Would you please help me to*

- accept and appreciate these breasts you've given me, even though they're _____
- know that it isn't just my breasts that make me female, that I am a girl through and through in spite of

_____

- not try to change my breasts by

  _____

- ignore the teasing and pray for the teasers, like

  _____

- not let any of this upset me so much that I miss out on the fun of becoming a young woman.

  Amen,

  _____ *(your name)*

Remember that God loves you, that he has plans for you, that he knows what you're going through to get there, and that he's here every step of the way. That's gotta help.

The perfect bra for me would look like and feel like....

_____

_____

_____

_____

_____

_____

_____

_____

_____

_____

_____

_____

The Whole Thing's Easier
If You Take Care of Yourself:
Diet

Then God said, "I give you every seed-bearing plant
on the face of the whole earth and every tree that has fruit
with seed in it. They will be yours for food."
Genesis 1:29

Could anything be more boring than reading about what foods you should eat?

Well, yeah. We could discuss the exports of Peru, or prime numbers, or today's interest rates . . .

There *are* less interesting things than food, and nutrition really *can* be fun to think about if you realize that the one thing that has more influence than anything else on the way you look and feel is your diet.

Besides—God says we need to think about it.

HOW IS THIS A God Thing?

In the Bible, there are literally *hundreds* of references to food, everything from what to eat—milk, butter, cheese, bread, corn, fish, flesh (relax—it means meat!), herbs, fruit, honey, oil, and vinegar!—to how to prepare it. From what *not* to eat—pig, badger, and camel (like we *would!*)—to how much to eat. From whom to eat with to where we sit at the table.

But Paul sums it up the best for us in Romans 14:17 when he says, "For the kingdom of God is not a matter of eating and drinking, but of righteousness, peace and joy in the Holy Spirit."

Food, he goes on to say in 1 Corinthians 8:8, doesn't bring us nearer to God. But the way we take care of our bodies *does* help us have a better relationship with God. "God's temple is sacred, and you are that temple" (1 Corinthians 3:17). You have to feed that body of yours right, or you aren't taking care of your temple.

Delicate Balance

You're growing right now—big time—so it's more important than ever to give yourself a mixture of all kinds of foods. The trick is to eat enough of the most nutritious foods—you know, the veggies and fruits and whole grains—and not too much of the stuff that's high in fat and sugar—the Snickers bars and the potato chips.

✓ CHECK Yourself OUT

Before we start this "quiz," you need to make sure you know what a *serving* is, since the questions ask you how many servings you eat of something a day. It's different with different foods, but this list of examples might give you a general idea:

BREAD—	1 slice
CEREAL—	1/2 cup
VEGGIES—	a pile about the size of your fist
APPLE—	1 medium sized
STRAWBERRIES—	1 cup
MILK—	1 cup
CHEESE—	1 hunk, golf ball size
HAMBURGER—	1 patty about the size of a deck of cards
M&M's—	one small handful

In each question, circle the number of servings you eat each day. Be honest, of course! You might have to pay attention to what you eat for a day before you can really answer. No one eats exactly the same thing every day, but try to think about what you put away during a typical twenty-four hour period.

1. **How many servings of bread, cereal, tortillas, rice, pasta, or any other kind of grain-thing do you eat every day?**

    10 9   8   7   6   5   4   3   2   1   0

2. **How many servings of veggies do you eat every day?**

    10 9   8   7   6   5   4   3   2   1   0

3. **How many servings of fruit do you eat every day, including juice with no added sugar?**

    10 9   8   7   6   5   4   3   2   1   0

4. **How many servings of dairy products like milk, cheese, cottage cheese, and yogurt do you eat every day?**

10   9   8   7   6   5   4   3   2   1   0

5. **How many servings of meat, including chicken and fish, do you eat every day?**

10   9   8   7   6   5   4   3   2   1   0

6. **How many servings of fats, oils, and sweets do you eat each day— things like candy, sodas, salad dressings, assorted junk food!**

10   9 8   7 6 5 4   3 2   1   0

Now take a look at the Food Pyramid and see how your eating habits fit. This pyramid, by the way, is recommended by some folks who devote their lives to helping people eat well.

Fats, Oils, Sweets

Meat & Protein

Milk

Fruit

Vegetable

Bread

Girlz WANT TO KNOW

❁ *SUZIE: I eat three meals a day like you're supposed to when you play sports and are active like I am, but I get way hungry between meals. I always heard I'd get fat if I ate between meals.*

Whoever said that was probably a couch potato! For most active girls, three squares are *not* enough to get you through the day. Pack a snack for midmorning, if you can squeeze it in, and one for after school. It isn't even a bad idea to have a glass of low-fat milk before you go to bed. As long as your snacks are healthy foods like fruit, cheese, yogurt, peanut butter— that kind of thing—you don't have to worry about "getting fat." You're burning a lot of calories in your on-the-go lifestyle.

✿ *ZOOEY: When I can't think of anything else to do, I go to the refrigerator and see what Mom's bought at the grocery store. Is that bad?*

Eating is never "bad" if you do it when you're hungry. It can hurt you, though, if you're eating just because you're bored or if your habit is to have a bag of chips and a soda every time you turn on the television or start your homework. Try eating only when you're hungry—and stopping when you're full. When you were little your parents probably told you to clean your plate, but now you have a better handle on how *you* feel. As long as you're not going to graze on junk food later, there's no need to lick the platter, especially if your stomach is telling you there's no more room.

✿ *KRESHA: Should I be taking vitamins, too?*

Most doctors agree that if you're eating a good diet—like the one recommended on the Food Pyramid—you don't really need vitamin supplements unless you have a proven deficiency in one of them. But knowing what the various vitamins do for you—and your beauty!—might encourage you to eat those healthy foods:

Vitamin A	gives you bright eyes and smooth skin and is found in yellow fruits, veggies, and spinach.
Vitamin B	provides energy and is found in meat, fish, poultry, leafy greenies, dried beans, and whole wheat foods.
Vitamin C	helps prevent colds and makes strong teeth and bones and great muscles and gums. It can be found in oranges, strawberries, broccoli, and spinach.

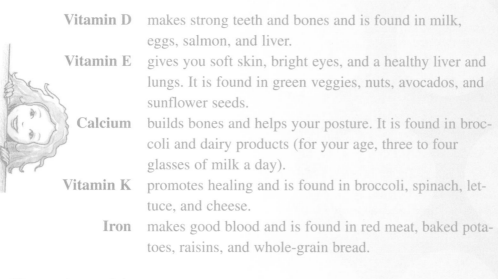

Vitamin D makes strong teeth and bones and is found in milk, eggs, salmon, and liver.

Vitamin E gives you soft skin, bright eyes, and a healthy liver and lungs. It is found in green veggies, nuts, avocados, and sunflower seeds.

Calcium builds bones and helps your posture. It is found in broccoli and dairy products (for your age, three to four glasses of milk a day).

Vitamin K promotes healing and is found in broccoli, spinach, lettuce, and cheese.

Iron makes good blood and is found in red meat, baked potatoes, raisins, and whole-grain bread.

Your Food 'Tude

Since we have to eat to live, what we eat is pretty important. We do need to think about it. On the other hand, we don't have to obsess! What you think about food is as important as what you eat, and when we're talking about attitude—the way you think and feel about something—you always need to go to God to make sure you're on the right track for you. Some things you might discuss with God in your next quiet time are

- being unhappy with the way your body looks
- eating too much
- not eating enough
- eating too much junk food
- not having a balanced diet at home
- not *liking* healthy food!
- feeling like a geek because you care about nutrition and none of your friends even give it a thought
- feeling so overwhelmed already, you don't have *time* to think about food, too

God wants you to be healthy, but he doesn't want this whole nutrition thing to be a drag. After all, he wants your mind clear for listening to him. So pray for his help in whatever way you need it. Ask in his name, and it shall be given—a healthy Food 'Tude. If you still have food issues, talk to your mom, and be sure to read chapter 8.

Just Do It

I promised you the food thing could be fun, so let's prove it. Below you'll find spaces for a day's worth of menus. Using the Food Pyramid to remind you what's in the various food groups, choose only things you *like* to fill in your menu. Then see if you can arrange to eat it soon. You'll be surprised how yummy eating healthy can be.

Breakfast
Bread group _____
Bread group _____
Fruit group _____
Milk group _____

Midmorning Snack
Bread group _____
Fruit group _____

Lunch
Bread group _____
Bread group _____
Veggie group _____
Milk group _____
Protein group _____

Afternoon Snack
Bread group _____
Bread group _____
Fruit group _____
Veggie group _____

Dinner

Bread group _____

Bread group _____

Veggie group _____

Veggie group _____

Milk group _____

Protein group _____

Now go back and add a little bit of fat to each meal (butter on your bread or salad dressing on your salad) and one sweet treat for the whole day. Enjoy!

Lily Pad

Describe your dream meal, from appetizer through dessert. Make your mouth water!

The Whole Thing's Easier
If You Take Care of Yourself:

Exercise

**She sets about her work vigorously;
her arms are strong for her tasks.**

Proverbs 31:17

Attention All Couch Potatoes!

Yeah, I know some of you are thinking, "Leave me alone! I *hate* playing sports. I'd rather curl up with a book. Besides, I'm not fat!"

Relax, ladies! Here's some good news for you:

- You don't have to play sports to get exercise.
- You can still spend plenty of time with that book.

And here's some *important* news for you—exercising isn't just about losing weight. It's about

- having energy to do the stuff you like to do
- sleeping better
- making your muscles stronger and more flexible (and you'll look better if they are!)
- strengthening your heart and yes, even at your young age you need to do that
- burning fat
- building your confidence *and*
- *taking care of that temple because, yes, it* is *a God thing.*

Okay, Okay, So I Need to Exercise–How Much?

✓ CHECK Yourself OUT

Circle the answer under each question that is the *closest* to sounding like you. Then we'll talk about what, if anything, you need to do to get yourself on the right exercise track.

1. **I do aerobic exercise (exercise that raises your heart rate and speeds up your breathing) . . .**

   A. Every day for at least two hours.

   B. About three times a week for at least twenty minutes.

   C. As little as possible!

2. **When I exercise, either by choice or by force (!), I breathe**

   A. So hard I can't talk while I'm exercising.

   B. Hard enough that I can't sing, but I can talk fairly easily.

   C. Just like normal because I don't exert myself unless I absolutely have to.

3. **When I'm exercising, I'm thinking about**

   A. How I'm doing, whether my heart rate is right, and how long I'm exercising.

   B. How much fun I'm having.

   C. When it's going to be over.

4. **In my daily activities, I**

   A. Keep moving all the time, hardly ever sitting down for very long.

   B. Move around a lot, but also enjoy being still once in a while.

   C. Move around as little as possible.

5. **If I have to go somewhere a few blocks from my house, I**

   A. Ride my bike at top speed or run.

   B. Walk.

   C. Get somebody to drive me.

6. **If I went on a two-mile hike today, I would**

   A. Probably beat everyone to the finish and barely be breathing hard.

   B. Probably be breathing harder than usual, but I'd have fun.

   C. Be half dead after the first mile.

Now take a look at the letters you circled. Figure out which letter you chose most often. Then look to see how that adds up.

If you circled mostly A's, you're definitely getting plenty of exercise—which is great. But pay attention to how your body feels while you're exercising or playing. If you hurt any place or you feel nauseated or your head starts to spin inside, stop right away and sit down. Those symptoms mean you're overdoing it. Listen to your thoughts, too. Are you really enjoying being so active that you barely sit down? If so, go for it, girl. If you can't honestly say you are, try looking at your many activities and see if you might let go of one or two to give yourself time to catch your breath. There is such a thing as *too much* exercise.

If you circled mostly B's, your fitness "plan" is right on target. You're getting enough exercise, and—maybe even more important—you're enjoying it. If you like what you're doing to keep your body fit, you're more likely to keep doing it—for life!

If you circled mostly C's, darlin', you need to get out of the recliner more often and get your body moving, even if you are currently stick woman. Maybe you aren't the athletic type, but that doesn't matter. You can walk the dog, ride your bike, get your friends together regularly and dance, climb trees. As long as you spend at least twenty minutes doing it three times a week so that your breathing and your heart rate speed up, you're benefiting from it. You might not be able to keep it up for twenty minutes at first, so go for ten, or even five, and build from there. I guarantee you, you'll feel better and you'll have more energy for the other things you like to do.

The Right Stuff in Exercise
Girlz WANT TO KNOW

✿ *LILY: I see a lot of older men—well, you know, in their thirties— doing all this stretching out before they run. Are they just showing off, or is it because they're old that they have to do that?*

Actually, it doesn't have anything to do with either age or impressing someone. You yourself should always stretch out your muscles before you do any kind of physical activity. Not only will it get you ready mentally for your workout, but it will help prevent injuries to your muscles, like pulls and tears which will put you out of commission for a while. The same goes for when you're finished. While your heart rate and breathing are slowing down, do some more gentle stretching. It will keep you from being stiff and sore the next day—and walking like an "old lady."

✿ *RENI: I was watching an old exercise video, and everybody on it was bouncing in their stretches. Are you supposed to do that?*

No! In fact, let's go over some guidelines for stretching:

- *Stretch really slowly.* An injury is not worth being the first one out on the volleyball court, right?
- *Don't bounce.* Bouncing was a popular move back in the '80s, but since then we've discovered that bouncing up and down can hurt your muscles.
- *Hold the stretch.* Once you're into a stretch, breathe deeply and count to ten. If that's too long at first, hold it as long as you can and work your way up to ten over a period of days.

✿ *SUZIE: My gymnastics coach makes us wear all these knee pads and things when we're learning a new move, but isn't that just because he'll get in trouble if any of us gets hurt? I don't have to do that when I'm working on my own, do I?*

You should. It's always better to be safe than sorry. When you're riding your bike, wear a helmet. When you're roller blading, wear wrist guards and bright clothes. When you're playing basketball, wear high tops. When you're practicing your sport on your own, wear the same protection gear your coach insists on at official practices and games. No one's trying to turn you into a wimp. Why get hurt if you can prevent it?

✿ *KRESHA: I love to go roller-skating at the rink, but every time I go, my mom makes me take a water bottle because she says I sweat so much. I feel like a geek hauling that around!*

But your mom's right. Your body keeps you cool by producing sweat, but you need to keep replacing those fluids with water before, during, and after you exercise. There are all kinds of really fun water bottles. Find one you really like—and drain it into your tummy often!

✿ *ZOOEY: I know I'm supposed to get exercise, but I'm a spastic. I'm so uncoordinated I always mess up the games and can never hit the ball or whatever, and everybody either laughs at me or yells at me because I'm making the team lose. I hate it!*

Maybe you will always be the one who cheers the team on from the sidelines—and that's okay. But you won't always be as uncoordinated as you feel right now. Your whole body is growing, but not all the parts are growing at the same time, which means your arms and legs won't do what you want them to, or you feel like you're all elbows and knees or just one big belly! You'll grow out of it, and in the meantime, exercise will help you become more in control of your body.

Don't want to get coordination training out there where everyone can tease you? I don't blame you! Start out doing something you can do by yourself, like walking or using an exercise tape at home. Or ask someone you trust not to poke fun at you to teach you how to play badminton or swim the backstroke. Although some people *are* more naturally athletic than others, everyone has to learn by doing. The more you do it, the better you'll get at it, and who knows? You might be out there playing volleyball with the team after all!

Just Do It

Let's play around with this whole fitness thing. On the one-week calendar below, fill in the physical activities you're already doing—soccer practices, dance classes, the five-minute walk home from school.

If you see that you're already exercising three times a week for twenty minutes at a time, pat yourself on the back and keep it up.

If you're *not* exercising three times a week for twenty minutes at a time, plan that kind of exercise and put it on your calendar. Don't forget to

- Do fun things—like dancing, no-brainer-no-skill games, and hiking to your favorite spot
- Do practical things—like walking to school, raking the yard, and riding your bike to your friends' houses
- Get someone to hold you accountable for keeping to your "exercise plan"
- Reward yourself when you've done it—eating a package of peanut M&Ms, reading your favorite book for the umpteenth time, or taking a nap in the hammock
- Do it again next week!

Talking to God About It

As always, pour out your "fitness issues" to God, and he'll listen to every word, no matter how lame it may sound coming out of your mouth! Tell him everything, and if you need some help getting started, try this approach:

Dear _____ (your favorite way to address God),

I really do want to take care of this temple of a body, because I know it's sacred to you. I wouldn't let the church building get all cobwebby and dusty if it were my responsibility to clean it, so I guess I can't let this temple go, either. But I'm going to need your help.

My biggest problem with exercising is

_____

_____.

*When it comes to exercising or playing sports, I hate being teased about*_____

_____.

When I think about sports and fitness and all that, I worry about

_____

_____.

While we're on the subject of fitness, God, I'm sorry that I

_____

_____.

Will you help me with

_____

_____?

Thank you for making my body

_____

_____.

I love you!

Lily Pad

If I could be a star in any physical activity—any at all—it would be

_____.

In fact, I can imagine it right now, in detail...

_____

_____

_____

_____

_____

_____

_____

_____

_____

_____

_____

_____

Don't Trash Your Temple

**You are not your own [but God's] .... Therefore
honor God with your body.**
1 Corinthians 6:19–20

HONOR GOD
WITH
YOUR BODY

You're at a point in your life when your parents aren't around you all the time anymore, and you're being influenced by many more people—teachers, school administrators, friends, older kids at your school, counselors, pastors— the list goes on. That's normal and healthy and helps make you a strong, well-rounded person.

But it can also present you with challenges, things you'll have to make decisions about, things that will make a difference in how you treat your body. You might have already made a vow to yourself never to let any of these things touch your body:

- cigarettes, cigars, tobacco of any kind
- alcohol
- illegal drugs, including marijuana

You might even have gone so far as to decide you're always going to have good sleep and eating habits. Maybe you're committed to protecting every part of you from harm. If you have, good for you!

But do keep in mind that even the strongest vow can become wobbly if

- everybody else is doing it
- everybody else seems to be having *fun* doing it
- everybody else seems so grown-*up* doing it
- you figure out it's *your* body and nobody else's—and you can realistically do whatever you want to it
- you realize your body is the only thing you *do* have control over right now, since everybody else controls your behavior and your time and where you live and . . .

You get the idea, don't you? It's downright hard out there in the world to keep the promises you've made to yourself *if* you don't go to God with those promises.

HOW IS THIS A God Thing?

We already know your body doesn't belong to just you—it belongs to you *and* God. Let's look at the whole passage from the quote at the beginning of this chapter, just to refresh your memory:

Don't you know that you yourselves are God's temple and that God's Spirit lives in you? If anyone destroys God's temple, God will destroy him; for God's temple is sacred, and you are that temple.
(1 Corinthians 6:19–20)

What we need to focus on now is how much we need God in order to remember that. The bottom line is *we can't do it without God!*

If you're going to say no to drugs when everybody who's anybody is doing them and enjoying them, you *have* to remember:

God is faithful; he will not let you be tempted beyond what you can bear. But when you are tempted, he will also provide a way out so that you can stand up under it.
(1 Corinthians 10:13)

If you're going to say no to alcohol when all the cool people are drinking it, you *must* keep in mind:

Submit yourselves, then, to God. Resist the devil, and he will flee from you.
(James 4:7)

If you're going to say no to that cigarette when you're really curious about what it's like to smoke one, you *gotta* remember what Jesus said:

Apart from me you can do nothing.
(John 15:5)

If you're going to go to sleep at a decent hour when that cute boy wants to talk half the night on the phone, or you're going to eat a healthy amount of food even though all the models in the magazines look like they starve themselves, or even for what seem like lesser temptations—please, please, please keep in mind:

**It is God who works in you to will and to act according
to his good purpose.**
(Philippians 2:13)

Work on your relationship with God every day, and he'll be there for you when your promises are put to the test. He'll help you say *no* in a way that may even help somebody else say no, too.

"Evils" We Don't Think About Much

You've probably been hearing about the evils of drugs, alcohol, and tobacco since you were in about third grade! But there are some other temptations adults may not have discussed with you. Let's take a peek at a few:

Could You Turn That Thing Down!

What teen or preteen *doesn't* like to listen to her music loud and clear?

But be careful. Loud music, especially coming through headphones, can damage your hearing over time. Once you lose it, you won't get it back. So next time you put your headphones on and crank up your music, have somebody stand beside you. If she can hear the music coming out of your phones, turn it down until she can't. You'll thank me later!

Night Owl!

Your body's rhythms—called **circadian rhythms**—may change at puberty, so that you find yourself wanting to stay up late at night and sleep in—way in!—in the morning. Unfortunately, most school schedules and other responsibilities don't work around that, so you need to establish a good sleep schedule and help yourself get to sleep on time—even if all your friends are smuggling their phones into their bedrooms and yakking until the wee hours, or if you'd rather stay up with a flashlight and read that great book than get the shut-eye you need for school. So . . .

✓ CHECK Yourself OUT

Are you getting enough sleep—and the right kind of sleep—and at the right time? Circle the answer to each question that best fits you.

1. I wake up in the morning

3 Pretty energetic and ready to go after a couple of minutes.

2 Sleepy, but I can function pretty well within a half hour.

1 Ready to blacken the eye of the person who woke me up; I don't really wake all the way up until about noon.

2. Every night I get

3 At least eight hours' sleep, and sometimes more.

2 Eight hours' sleep, and sometimes a little less.

1 Way less than eight hours' sleep.

3. The amount of sleep I get

3 Is almost the same every night, no matter what day of the week it is or what time of year.

2 Is the same every night during the week during school, but it varies on the weekends and during vacations.

1 Is different just about every night.

4. I go to sleep

3 Almost as soon as my head hits the pillow, or at least within fifteen minutes.

2 Pretty soon after I go to bed, although sometimes I lie awake for maybe a half hour or an hour.

1 Hours after I go to bed (or am supposed to go to bed); sometimes I lie awake half the night, it seems like.

5. **When I sleep**

   3 An atomic bomb could drop and I wouldn't wake up.

   2 I don't wake up until morning unless there's a lot of commotion or something.

   1 I wake up a lot, sometimes with nightmares or because I'm worried or something scares me.

Now add up your score of circled numbers: _____

Before we go on, let me remind you that no score is "bad." Some scores just mean you might want to pay attention to some things, just to be sure you're getting all the rest you need to be happy, healthy—beautiful!

If your score is between 13 and 15, you're a pretty efficient sleeper, and you seem to be on a good schedule. Keep up those good habits of sticking to a regular bedtime and getting at least eight hours' sleep if not more every night. You're doing a lot to keep your body healthy.

If your score is between 9 and 12, you have some good sleep habits, but if you want to really be at your best, look at your "2" and "1" answers. Can you work on some of those areas? For help with how, read the hints under the next score range.

If your score is between 5 and 8, you're being cheated out of feeling your best by what we call sleep deprivation. It's probably not your "fault." We can't just turn off a switch that renders us asleep until the next morning! But there are some ways you can help yourself get the rest you need:

- Go to bed and get up at the same time every day, no matter what day of the week or what time of year. Once you start sleeping better, you can give yourself the occasional sleep-in treat.
- Get a routine going that you follow every night before you go to bed, and do that same thing every night. Maybe you'll take a hot bath, crawl into bed with your journal, turn on some music, and take fifteen or twenty minutes to unwind. Some girls like tapes with nature sounds. Others like to read a couple of paragraphs before they doze off. Try not to make your ritual sacking out in front of the TV.
- Exercise regularly, but don't do it within an hour or two of bedtime.

- Don't drink or eat anything with caffeine after about 8:00 p.m. That means sodas, coffee, tea, and chocolate.
- Don't eat a big meal within an hour or two of bedtime, either. On the other hand, if your tummy's growling at bedtime, drink a glass of milk.
- If you're worried or excited about something before you go to bed, try talking it out with someone or writing about it in your journal before you hit the sack.
- Never go to bed all wound up. Do some gentle stretching, take a hot bath, rock in a rocker. There's nothing worse than getting into bed and flopping like a flounder because you can't get settled down!
- If you can't sleep night after night, or you're plagued with nightmares every night, talk to your mom and dad. Parents, a doctor, or a counselor can help you, so don't let not sleeping well go on without telling someone. Life is too much fun for you to be too tired to enjoy it.

By the way—if bed-wetting is a sleep problem for you, don't feel alone. *Enuresis*, as it's called, happens to a lot of girls—guys, too. It's because your bladder is too small to hold all the urine your body makes during the night. Don't despair! You'll grow out of it. Meanwhile, your doctor can give you one of several different kinds of medicines to keep it from being a problem. There's hope for those sleep-overs yet!

Food Nightmares

You've probably heard of eating disorders like anorexia and bulimia. Even if you have, they're so dangerous it's worth running over them one more time.

Eating Disorders in General

When a girl becomes so obsessed with losing weight that she stops eating normally, chances are she has an eating disorder. No matter how thin she is, when she looks in a mirror she sees a fat girl. She may go from eating less and less to throwing up what she does eat, taking too many laxatives, swallowing diet pills, and exercising until she drops. Unless she gets help, she'll get sick. She could damage her body permanently or even die. It's that serious.

Anorexia

A girl who has anorexia nervosa will basically try to starve herself. She thinks about avoiding food all the time. When she does eat, she uses certain "rituals" to keep from eating what she considers too much—doing things like cutting her food up into small pieces so it looks like she's eaten, eating very slowly, not touching her mouth with the fork, or playing with her food. As she gets thinner and thinner, she starts having physical problems and may have to be hospitalized. Usually it takes intense counseling of some kind to get a girl with anorexia back to healthy eating.

Bulimia

A girl with bulimia also wants to be thin, but she tries to accomplish this by eating a whole *bunch* of food in a short period of time (that's called binge-ing) and then forcing herself to throw it all up—day after day after day. She, too, will become ill if she doesn't get help, and she'll suffer from stomach-aches, sore throats, and even tooth decay.

When to Get Help

A lot of the things we've talked about in this book have been just a normal part of growing into a young woman. Other things aren't, like

- sincere hatred of your own body
- menstrual cramps that put you in bed or keep you from your normal activities
- periods that last longer than eight days or occur less than twenty-one days apart

- severe overweight
- an addiction to drugs, alcohol, or cigarettes
- extreme insomnia (not being able to sleep)
- anorexia
- bulimia

If you're experiencing any of these things, you *really* need to talk to your parents about getting some help. There's no shame in going to a doctor or a counselor. In fact, being willing to reach out for help shows real maturity in you. Know that God does *not* want puberty to be a miserable experience for you, and he sure doesn't want you to suffer alone. As always, pour out your problems to him. Every challenge has a solution. Always.

Just Do It

We've been talking about some heavy stuff in this chapter. Let's lighten up and look at your blessings—what do you say? A look at how very good your life is can help you steer clear of the pitfalls.

- One thing I love about my family is _____.
- One thing I love about my best friend is _____.
- My favorite part of the day is when _____.
- I'd rather eat _____ than anything.
- I love to go to _____.
- I love to wear _____.
- I feel loved when _____.
- I can't wait to _____.
- The thing I love best about God is _____.
- I know God loves me because _____.

Doesn't that feel great? You have a lot going for you, girl. Don't waste an ounce of it on things that aren't good for you.

Lily Pad

If I had a friend who had a problem that was hurting her, I would...

_____
_____
_____
_____
_____
_____
_____
_____
_____
_____

A Final Send-Off

A kindhearted woman gains respect.
Proverbs 11:16

Remember About God-Confidence?

If you've read *The Beauty Book,* you might remember us talking about the kind of confidence that makes you beautiful. It's the same kind of confidence that makes you glowing and healthy, that makes you want to take care of and respect your unique body. Let's review.

Have you ever known a girl who wasn't "with" the rest of the girls when it came to her development? You know, maybe she didn't have a sign of a breast or she had enough breasts for three people? And yet the more you got to know her, the cooler she seemed because not only did she respect everyone and treat them more than decently, but she treated herself the same way?

You look good when you *are* good. You look beautiful when you are sure of yourself—and you feel beautiful, too. A lot of people call that *self-confidence.* It's really *God-confidence.*

✓ CHECK Yourself OUT

See for yourself. Stand in front of a mirror. Smile at that girl looking back at you as if you like her and accept her and want to be best friends. Now watch what happens when you look at her as if you hate her guts. Which girl looks better, no matter what her breasts or her skin or her waistline is doing?

HOW IS THAT A God Thing?

You can have that God-confidence that makes you beautiful and mature because

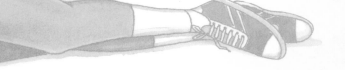

89

- God carefully chose each of your features and combined them to make *you*
- God's idea of you is perfect, even if the going look for models doesn't agree
- Jesus talked only about inner beauty, and if you got him, you've got that, baby!

Now might be a good time to stop reading and just say thank you to him.

It's a Lifelong Thing

We've also been talking about all this body-care and upkeep as if it were a puberty-thing. But the stuff we've covered is stuff you'll need to pay attention to your whole life:

- understanding what's happening inside your body at any given time— like when you get married, when you're pregnant, after you've had a baby, and when you're starting menopause (which is kind of like the reverse of puberty!)
- paying attention to your body's signals
- liking and respecting your body
- nurturing yourself when your period gives you a bad time
- wearing comfortable bras
- eating a nutritious diet
- getting the right amount of exercise
- avoiding cigarettes, illegal drugs, and the abuse of alcohol
- getting the right amount of sleep
- not obsessing about weight so much that you hurt yourself
- getting the help you need if your struggles become more than you can handle
- always having another woman you can trust to talk to
- going to God with everything and knowing he's there for you

If that way of living becomes second nature to you now, you're going to have a life that is so much happier, healthier, and problem-free than it would be if you didn't develop these good habits. This is forever we're talking about, and forever starts right now!

The Bennies

Just in case you aren't yet convinced that your body is worth all this attention, let's list the benefits in plain, practical language:

- bright eyes that see the world as only you can
- sharp ears that can hear all the world's best sounds, including the voices of the people you love
- a sound, alert mind that can stay focused on God and show you how to live the glorious life he has planned for you
- a clear voice that can tell it to the world
- the strength and energy to do all that God asks you to—you'll never have to offer some lame excuse
- a heart that beats with kindness and respect and God-confidence
- a body that's ready to do all that God calls you to do as a woman, to be the best you can be

A Private Word

Just a final word before I leave you—and that's about privacy.

As you become more and more aware of your body, reserve the right to keep it private, even from your own family. This list might help you see what I mean:

- It's perfectly normal for you to want to keep your bedroom door closed when you're changing clothes or when you just want to be alone. If you share a room, it's still normal to want some private space somewhere.

- You shouldn't have to endure people coming into the bathroom when you're in the tub or on the toilet if you don't want them there.

- It isn't a sign of something wrong with you if you feel shy or self-conscious changing clothes or showering even in front of your best friends. Some people are more modest than others. Respect what makes you comfortable.

- If you have to see a doctor for any of your physical problems—especially a gynecologist, who specializes in women-stuff—you have the right to ask someone to explain to you exactly what's going to happen and even to request a female doctor if that would make you more comfortable.

- If a person touches you in a way that makes you feel uncomfortable, no matter who it is, tell an adult you trust *immediately*. Don't try to protect someone who is hurting you. Your body is yours and God's—keep it as protected and as private as you want to.

✓ CHECK Yourself OUT

All right, girl, let's take one last quiz to see where you are now that you've read all about puberty and had a lot of your questions answered. You might even want to come back and take this little checkup once every couple of months. You'll be surprised at how much you'll change—how much you'll grow—how close you'll constantly get to being—a *woman!*

See how many of these you can check off as the way you think. Don't check any you don't truly do or believe yet. The blanks will show you what things to keep working on.

_____ My body tells me when it's hungry, thirsty, tired, or sick—and I take care of it.

_____ When it comes to keeping clean, I'm there! I shower or bathe every day.

_____ Exercise is something I do a lot. It makes me feel great.

_____ When people talk about drugs, alcohol, and smoking being bad for your body, I agree because I know that stuff'll hurt me.

_____ If somebody touched me in a way I didn't want to be touched, I'd tell an adult I trust.

_____ I don't compare myself to the way other girls I know are developing.

_____ If I could change one thing about my body, I wouldn't do it. I'm me.

_____ I eat a pretty healthy diet most of the time, even when I'm not at home.

_____ I'm okay with the whole period thing.

_____ I get plenty of sleep.

_____ I have my moods, but they don't control me.

_____ I'm a girl and I love it!

_____ I know God has a plan for me, and I'm keeping myself in the best shape possible so I can carry it out.

_____ I go to God all the time for help with all of the above!

Lily Pad

If I had a little sister who wanted to know what it was like being an almost-woman like me, I'd tell her...

We want to hear from you. Please send your comments about this book to us in care of the address below. Thank you.

Zonder**kidz** ™

Grand Rapids, MI 49530
http://www.zonderkidz.com